Bobby Brewster's torch

Through his appearances on television, and
the story-telling sessions he has held in
libraries, schools and at parties in Australia,
New Zealand and South Africa as well as in
almost every part of Britain, H. E. Todd can
claim to be the best-known story-teller in the
world.

Here are ten stories about his favourite
character, Bobby Brewster, the boy to whom
the most extraordinary things happen.

H. E. TODD

Bobby Brewster's torch

Illustrated by Lilian Buchanan

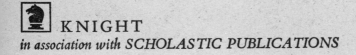

KNIGHT
in association with SCHOLASTIC PUBLICATIONS

ISBN 0 340 16055 1

This edition published by Knight Books,
the paperback division of Brockhampton Press Ltd, Leicester
Printed and bound in Great Britain by Cox & Wyman Ltd, Reading

First published 1969 by Brockhampton Press Ltd
Second Impression 1970

Text copyright © 1968 H. E. Todd
Illustrations copyright © 1969 Brockhampton Press Ltd

Contents

The flashing torch   *page* 9

Bobby Brewster by a tree   19

Pirate at the party   29

Sparrows in the letter-box   39

Talking to the wind   45

The suitcase   52

The think balloons   58

Undressed and in bed   67

The whistling golf-ball   75

The kite   84

Introduction

Once again I have to thank a lot of friends for helping me with this book. The letters that they wrote to me were very useful indeed. Here are their names: David Bryan, Angus Cameron, Sarah Clarke, Susan Daynes, Frances Douglas, Judith Emmett, Stephen Evans, Kevin Fortey, Pauline Greenwood, David Gudgeon, Emma Haggas, Hugh Jones, Jane Merrow-Smith, Jackie Myhill, Valerie Oakes, Jane Richards, Carole Savage, Karen Smith, Ian Sutcliffe, Ian Wakeling, Karen Wooster, and a number of friends at Loreto Convent Primary School, Omagh, Northern Ireland.

H. E. TODD

The flashing torch

Don't you think that Father Christmas is clever?
I do. The way he finds out exactly what you
want for Christmas, and then, if you haven't
been too greedy, nearly always gives it to you.
How on earth does he remember all the things
that everybody wants? I wish I had a memory
like his.

It was the year before last when Bobby
Brewster decided that he wanted a torch – and
that is putting it mildly. In early November,

when the dark evenings set in, he first thought that it would be rather nice to have a torch, but by the middle of December he was absolutely frantic for a torch and hardly ever talked about anything other than torches. The Brewsters had torch for breakfast, torch for dinner, torch for tea, and torch for supper. Whenever Bobby went shopping for his mother he took far longer than necessary, because he always stopped outside every electrical shop to gaze at the torches. Perhaps it was not surprising that Father Christmas got to hear about it.

On Christmas Eve Bobby went to bed early so that the next day would come all the sooner. Have you ever tried that? It works if you go to sleep quickly, and Bobby fell at once into a lovely dream. Do you know what the dream was about? Torches.

But even in his wildest dreams he could never have imagined what was in store for him on Christmas Day. He woke in the dark at about five o'clock in the morning with an excited Christmas feeling in his tummy. As he groped by the side of his bed for the light switch, he put his hand on the bedside table and felt an exciting metal object. Can you guess what it was? A torch.

Not an ordinary torch. Oh dear me no. It was shaped like a lantern, with a handle on top to carry it and a round glass window sticking out at the front. Bobby pressed a switch on the side and a fierce beam of white light shone across to the opposite side of his bedroom. He turned it towards the end of his bed, and there hung a pillow-case crammed full with presents. What absolute bliss! There was no need to switch on the bedroom light now. He could inspect his presents by the light of his lovely new torch.

Splendid presents they were, too, but I won't describe them all now because it would take too long. They looked extra exciting by torchlight, and when Bobby had opened all the parcels, stacked them tidily on the table, and folded up the paper wrapping, he looked more closely at his new torch. It was then that he had his biggest thrill so far. On the top of the torch was a red dome, and on the side, next to the main switch, was a second switch coloured red. He pressed it, and do you know what happened? A red light shone in the dome. But it didn't just shine. Oh dear me no. It flashed on and off like the flashing lights on top of a fire-engine or a police car. Bobby lay back in his bed thinking about all his presents and watching in fascination as the flashing red light made weird shadows on the walls of his bedroom. For a time he was in a wonderland all of his own.

Then he realized that the flashes were not

regular. They were short and long, like dots and dashes, but dots and dashes all mixed up without any regular pattern. When he had seen enough mixed-up red dots and dashes he jumped quietly out of bed, ran to the window, and shone his torch outside. A strong beam of light picked out the very topmost branch of the tallest tree in the garden. It did, really. And when he turned it down and shone it along the road it was even better. It threw a distinct patch of light on the railway bridge right by the side of the station. Wasn't that exciting?

But the most exciting thing of all happened later on Christmas Day. In the middle of tea Bobby suddenly asked his mother if for a special treat they could finish tea by torchlight.

'All right, Bobby,' said his mother. 'As long as you don't mind using up the battery.'

So out went the dining-room light and Bobby pressed the main switch of his torch. And just to make it more impressive he pressed the red switch as well. There sat the Brewsters drinking cups of tea and eating Christmas cake, with a beam of light shining from the torch on the table and the red dome flashing. It was like a scene in a pantomime. Then Mr Brewster discovered that it was even more marvellous than they thought.

'Why Bobby,' he said, 'those red flashes are not just dots and dashes. They're Morse code.'

'What's Morse code?' asked Bobby.

'It's what we used for sending and receiving messages when I was in the R.A.F.,' said his father. 'Keep quiet for a moment while I try to read it.'

They all sat as still as statues as Mr Brewster read out the message as the torch flashed each letter.

.-A

....H .-A .---P .---P .---Y

-...C ....H .-.R ..I ...S -T --M .-A ...S

'Gracious me, Bobby,' cried Mr Brewster, 'your torch is wishing us a happy Christmas!'

Bobby held his torch up by the handle, looked straight into its front window, and said distinctly –

'Happy Christmas, torch.'

Then the red flashes in the dome started again, and Mr Brewster read out the reply –

```
·-A ··N-··D
-T ····H·E
···S·-A--M·E
-T---O
-····Y---O ···-U
```

'That settles it,' said Bobby Brewster. 'Father Christmas has given me a magic torch.'

And on Boxing night the torch proved to be not only magic magic, but useful magic as well. As usual the Brewsters went to spend the afternoon and evening with some friends who live a few miles away, and they drove there in the car. Of course Bobby took his new torch with him, not only to help light the way home at night, but also to show off because he was so proud of it. The party didn't finish until late at night, and half-way home, to Mr Brewster's horror, the car suddenly stopped.

'Oh dear,' he said, 'whatever's the matter?'

He jumped out and opened the bonnet of the car. 'Shine your torch inside the bonnet for me please,' he asked. Bobby did as he was asked. Not that it helped much. Between you and me, Mr Brewster doesn't know anything about car engines and his looking inside the bonnet was a complete waste of time. As Bobby held up his torch by the handle he pushed the red switch as well and the red light started to flash. Mr Brewster was still busy looking inside the bonnet and Bobby was gazing along the road, so they took no particular notice of the flashes. But the driver of an approaching car did. He drew up on the other side of the road and jumped out.

'Hullo, old man, can I help?' he said. 'I see you need some petrol.'

'Do I?' asked Mr Brewster, taking his head out of the car bonnet.

'Yes,' said the man. 'Luckily I have a spare can in the back. Open your tank and I'll pour it in.' So they did. Then Bobby's father got back into the driver's seat, pressed the starter, and the engine started straight away.

'Thanks very much,' he said. 'I'm most obliged to you. But, tell me, how did you know I had run out of petrol?'

The man looked rather surprised at the question.

'From your message,' he said.

16

'What message?' asked Mr Brewster.

The man looked even more puzzled. 'Why, the message you were flashing with your torch, of course,' he explained. 'Luckily I can read Morse code, and as I was driving towards you I could see the red light flashing, "S.O.S. Petrol – S.O.S. Petrol – S.O.S. Petrol".'

'Oh, I see now,' said Mr Brewster, looking hard at Bobby. 'That explains it.' And the man seemed satisfied.

But I think it only half explained it, don't you? It explained why the man stopped and helped so kindly – but how on earth in the first place did Bobby Brewster's torch know that his father had run out of petrol?

Only the Brewsters themselves – and you and I – know the answer to that question.

Because Bobby Brewster's torch is magic.

Bobby Brewster by a tree

One fine Saturday morning last summer Bobby Brewster decided, for some odd reason, to take his paintbox out into the garden and paint a picture. I say 'for some odd reason' because in fact Bobby can't paint very well, and so he doesn't often try unless he is painting during lessons at school.

In the Brewsters' garden there is a remarkable tree. It is a spruce tree, and most of the branches spread proudly upwards, except for one that hangs in a peculiar way almost down to the ground. Bobby has always been interested in that particular tree, and has thought that the hanging branch looks like an arm, especially as at the bottom there is a bunch of green twigs shaped just like a hand. He thought that this tree might make a good subject for his painting, so he drew the garden table up towards it, sat down on a chair, and dipped his paintbrush in the water. Before starting on the actual picture he wrote in bold letters of black paint at the bottom of the page –

A TREE

BY BOBBY BREWSTER

He probably did that because he wanted to be quite sure that people would know what the picture was meant to be when he had finished it. There have been occasions in the past when it has been rather difficult to tell. Once, for instance, I congratulated him for painting such a lovely picture of a cat and he was quite upset because it was supposed to be a horse.

Anyway, he painted his tree and then added a picture of himself standing beside it. To be quite honest, the painting wasn't much like the tree and even less like him, as he stood back to admire it. But not for long, because a very funny thing happened.

A voice said, 'I don't think much of that.' It did, really.

'I beg your pardon?' asked Bobby Brewster.

'I said I don't think much of your painting of me,' said the voice.

'My painting of *you*?' asked Bobby in amazement. 'Do you mean to stand there in the middle of our garden and tell me you're a talking tree?'

'I do indeed,' said the tree. 'And let me tell you something else. If I really thought I looked like your painting of me, I would take jolly good care next winter time to wither right away and die. It's an insult. That's what it is. An insult!'

'I'm very sorry,' said Bobby. 'I did my best, but I'm afraid I'm not very good at painting pictures.'

'You're telling me,' said the tree. 'Why, I could do better myself.'

'That's ridiculous,' said Bobby. 'How could a tree paint a picture? For one thing, you haven't got any arms and hands.'

'Oh yes I have,' said the tree. 'What do you think this is?' And he waved the branch that looked like an arm and wiggled the twigs that looked like the fingers of a hand.

'That's a low hanging branch with some green twigs on the end,' said Bobby.

'Oh no it isn't,' said the tree. 'It's my arm and hand.'

'That's even more ridiculous,' cried Bobby.

'I wish you wouldn't keep calling me ridiculous,' said the tree crossly. 'I don't think you really mean it, but you can sound extremely rude sometimes. First of all you paint that insulting picture of me, and then you refuse to believe a word I say. As I said before, I *am* a magic tree. I *have* got an arm and hand. And I *can* paint a better picture than you can. And if you will push your table closer to me, with the paintbox and water and a clean sheet of paper on it, I will jolly well prove it to you.'

Bobby did as the tree had suggested, but

he still didn't really believe what it had told him.

'To start with,' he asked, 'how can you possibly pick up the paintbrush?'

'I don't *need* your rotten old paintbrush,' said the tree. 'I can use what you refuse to believe is my hand.'

And at that moment a very funny thing happened. The wind blew, the branches of the tree rustled, and the long overhanging arm with its green fingers outstretched swept into the water, on to the paintbox, and then across the clean page of paper. Bobby leant forward and distinctly saw the beginnings of the painting of a tree. And the extraordinary thing was that because the hand was so large, it had been able to use several different colours, and what is more they were exactly the right colours.

'Don't interrupt me,' said the tree sharply. 'Step aside please. I haven't finished painting myself yet,' and it made several more sweeps across the paintbox and paper.

'Now comes the difficult part,' said the tree. 'I'm going to paint you, and people are always awkward things to paint. Stand perfectly still while I look at you.'

Bobby stood like a statue. The arm of the tree moved again, and the hand made some squiggles across the paper.

'There you are,' said the tree proudly. 'What do you think of that?'

Bobby stepped forward and looked at the picture. 'Why, it's *marvellous*,' he cried. And it was. The tree was in the background of the picture, and very well painted it was, too. But even more remarkable was the painting of Bobby Brewster himself. It was a wonderful likeness. He could hardly believe his eyes.

'Now for the signature,' said the tree, and it dipped a single twig finger into the black paint and swept it boldly across the bottom of the page, finishing with a proud dot. Do you know what it had written?

BOBBY BREWSTER BY A TREE.

It had, really. And what is more the writing looked exactly the same as Bobby Brewster's writing on the bottom of his picture of the tree.

As Bobby stood looking in amazement at the

painting, his mother came out of the house without his even noticing her. And when *she* looked at the two pictures on the table she was even more amazed than he had been.

'Why Bobby,' she cried. 'The picture of you standing in front of the tree is easily the best thing you have ever done. It's *much* better than that of the tree standing by you. They don't even look as if they have been painted by the same person.'

Bobby was about to say, 'They haven't,' but then he paused. If he tried to explain that the better picture had actually been painted by the

BOBBY BREWSTER BY A TREE.

tree, he thought that his mother might think him silly. And I don't blame him, do you? And anyway, the words BOBBY BREWSTER BY A TREE might just as well be the title of the picture as the signature. So he kept quiet.

But he wasn't prepared for his mother's great enthusiasm. During the weekend she insisted on showing that picture to everyone who came to the house, and people kept patting Bobby on the back and telling him what a clever boy he was until he got positively sick of it. Then, to make matters worse, she went with Bobby to school on Monday morning and took the painting with her to give to Miss Trenham the headmistress.

'Are you *quite* sure that nobody helped him with this?' asked Miss Trenham, when Bobby had gone to his classroom.

'Positive,' said Mrs Brewster. 'He was out in the garden all by himself.'

'Well, it's a remarkable self-portrait,' said Miss Trenham. 'I shall really have to exhibit it in the school hall.'

So she did. And all the mistresses and masters and children at school patted Bobby on the back and told him what a clever boy he was until his poor back became very sore. After a time he simply couldn't stand it any longer, so he quietly went to talk to Mr Limcano during lunch time when he was alone in his classroom. Now, perhaps you know, Mr Limcano is a very nice man who is a bit of a magician himself, so magic doesn't surprise him as much as it would surprise most people.

'Sir,' asked Bobby Brewster, 'have you seen my painting in the school hall?'

'I have indeed,' said Mr Limcano, 'and I don't want to make you swollen-headed, but it is the most remarkable piece of work I have ever seen from a boy of your age.'

'Well, sir, it wasn't exactly painted by a boy of my age,' said Bobby. 'You see, it's a magic picture.'

'Exactly how magic is it?' asked Mr Limcano.

'The tree *painted* it, sir,' said Bobby.

'I beg your pardon?' asked Mr Limcano.

'I said that the picture was painted *by* the tree,' explained Bobby. 'That's what the words at the bottom mean. "BOBBY BREWSTER BY A

27

TREE." It doesn't mean BOBBY BREWSTER STANDING BY A TREE. It means BOBBY PAINTED BY A TREE.'

Mr Limcano looked keenly at Bobby for a moment. Then he spoke.

'Thank you for telling me, Bobby,' he said. 'But if that's really the case, I think we should keep quiet about it. You and I know all about magic, don't we? But if you start telling that story to other people they will never believe you.'

So Bobby did not say a word to anyone else, and that's really the end of the story. From that day to this Bobby has never painted anything very clever himself, and the magic tree has never talked again. But Bobby is still living in hopes. And just to keep his hopes alive, every morning, after he has dressed, he goes straight out into the garden, walks over to the tree, shakes it by the green twig hand, and says, 'Good morning, tree. Thank you for that lovely painting.'

Which is the least he can do, isn't it?

Pirate at the party

The invitation arrived one Saturday morning by post, and this is what it said:

'*Dear Bobby Brewster,*

 You are invited to a fancy-dress party at Crows-foot Farm on Saturday October 15th. Please be sure to arrive in time for the parade sharp at 4 pm.

     Yours sincerely,

     Angus Cameron.'

R.S.V.P.

'What does R.S.V.P. mean?' Bobby asked his mother.

'Will you please answer this letter,' replied Mrs Brewster.

'Then why doesn't it say so?' said Bobby. 'Of course I shall answer the letter. I shall say, "Thank you very much. I shall be delighted to come." '

So he did.

Then Bobby had to decide what fancy dress to wear. His mother said that she would make it for him, but she secretly hoped he wouldn't choose anything difficult. She needn't have worried. Bobby had no intention of going to the party as a gnome or an elf, because he thinks they are silly. Besides, he would have been paired off with some little girl who had gone as a fairy or a pixie, and he thinks fairies and pixies are even sillier than gnomes and elves. Nor did he want to go as anyone historical like Henry the Eighth or the King of Siam. Henry the Eighth would have to wear a beard, which would get in the way of the sardine sandwiches at tea, and the King of Siam might be expected to speak Siamese, which he didn't know. In the end, to Mrs Brewster's great relief, he said he would go as a pirate.

'That's easy,' said Mrs Brewster. 'You can wear your blue jeans tucked inside your wellington boots, and a roll-necked pullover. I'll embroider a skull and crossbones on your chest, and make you a pirate hat out of paper. Then we can put that old leather belt round your waist and punch an extra hole to pull it tight.'

'What about a cutlass?' asked Bobby. 'Can I use the garden scythe?'

No, you certainly can't,' said Mrs Brewster. 'You know perfectly well that I've told you never to touch it because it's dangerous. We'll make a cutlass out of cardboard and cover it with silver paper.'

'But that won't cut anything,' protested Bobby.

'And a jolly good thing too,' said his mother.

The clothes and equipment were all collected together, and early on the afternoon of Saturday October 15th Bobby dressed for the party. He was so anxious to get started that he was ready by half past two, and as it takes no more than a quarter of an hour to walk to Crowsfoot Farm, and less by car, there was plenty of time to spare.

'Can I go outside and play at pirates?' Bobby asked his mother.

'No, you certainly can't,' she said. 'The ground's wet and muddy and you'll only get in

a state. Sit down quietly and read a nice book.'

Bobby didn't want to sit down quietly and read a nice book. But he found one called *Bold Ben Blister the Pirate* and read a very exciting chapter about boarding a Spanish man-of-war, seizing the gold bullion, and slaughtering all the crew. I don't know whether you'd call that a nice book, but he did. He imagined himself as Bold Ben Blister, and swished his cutlass about in a most menacing manner. Then he noticed from the pictures that Ben Blister had a tattooed arm, so he turned up the sleeve of his pullover and painted a black skull and crossbones on his left wrist. Most lifelike it was, too, if it's possible for a skull and crossbones to be lifelike.

All that took time, and he had to wait for the tattooing to dry before he could hide it with his sleeve. Then he had an idea, and ran downstairs.

'Mother,' he said, in a polite and helpful sort of voice, 'there's no need for you to bother to drive me to the party. I can easily walk there, and you'll have to fetch me when it's over, so it'll save you the trouble of taking the car out twice.'

Mrs Brewster looked doubtful. 'Are you quite sure you won't feel silly walking there dressed as a pirate?' she asked.

'Perfectly sure,' said Bobby. 'There won't be many people about on the way to the farm anyway.'

'Well,' said Mrs Brewster, 'I *am* in the middle of a job that I should like to finish. Very well, you may start in ten minutes. But don't do anything silly.'

'Of course not,' said Bobby. 'As if I would.'

He ran upstairs in delight to fetch his pirate hat and cutlass. The other boys would have to go to the party with their mothers and be given a last-minute tidying up in the hall of the farm, wouldn't they? But not Bobby Brewster. He was going all by himself, and he could pretend to be a real pirate.

There was one difficult thing to decide. How *would* a real pirate arrive at a party? After all, no one in his right senses would ever invite a real pirate to a party, anyway, so he would have to *force* his way in.

'That's what I'll do,' said Bobby Brewster to himself. 'I'll board Crowsfoot Farm through a window, like a real pirate storming a ship.'

The best path for hiding on the way led over a stile, through a small wood, over a fence, and then by a pond. And that's where the trouble started. The first thing that happened was that Bobby slipped when getting over the stile and fell on his chest, so his skull and crossbones were covered with mud. That didn't matter much, but there was worse to come. His pirate hat was caught by an overhanging branch. This tore it and tossed it upwards to a higher branch where Bobby couldn't reach it. So there he was, a pirate without a skull and crossbones or a hat. Then he didn't notice a strand of barbed wire at the bottom of the gate, so he tore a ragged hole in his jeans and caught his pullover as well.

But his worst misfortune came last. In a fit of enthusiasm he swished his cutlass through the air and yelled, 'Avaunt, ye lubbers!' – or words to that effect. By mistake he let go of the cutlass which flew through the air and landed plonk in the pond. Bobby leant over the pond to fish it out with a stick, and, can you guess? He fell in. His hands and face were covered with mud, and

his knee, too, through the hole in his jeans. You never saw such a sight. And, even more awkward, when he fished the cutlass out of the water, it was all soggy and shapeless and the silver paper had peeled off and floated away. So now he was a very muddy pirate without a skull and cross-bones, a hat, or a cutlass!

By this time it was getting late. Bobby Brewster ran to the front door of the farm and rang the bell. He decided not to climb through the window and smear everything with mud, and I think that was very wise of him, don't you?

Mrs Cameron came to the door. 'Why, Bobby,' she said to the dirty object standing in front of her, 'What a *marvellous* costume. You're just in time for the parade. Run through to the sitting-room at once.'

Bobby felt rather puzzled, but there was no time to waste, so he ran and joined the parade.

Mr and Mrs Cameron had asked a lady without any children of her own to do the judging, because they thought that would be fairer. First of all the children had to walk round and round in a circle. Then they stood one by one in front of the judge so that she could look at them properly. Bobby Brewster felt an awful fool when he was standing there, especially as the mud on his face and hands had dried and started to crack. The judge asked the children to stand quietly while she thought hard.

'Well, children,' she announced at last, 'you all look wonderful in your costumes, and it is very difficult to decide which is the best. I'm going to give the prize to the one who I think is the most original. Bobby Brewster. It was a splendid idea to come as a tramp. I've never seen a more realistic tramp in my life, so he wins the prize.'

Bobby was too surprised to say anything while everyone was clapping. He was just going to explain, 'But I'm *not* a tramp. I'm a pirate,' when Mrs Cameron took him by the arm and said, 'Well done, Bobby, and now I think you'd better go and wash before tea.' And she led him firmly up to the bathroom and gave him a towel and some soap. As you can imagine, when the party was over and the Camerons were tired out with washing up afterwards, they were not very

37

pleased to have to go upstairs and clean up the bathroom as well.

That's not quite the end of the story. When Bobby arrived home that evening after the party, he felt rather ashamed about the extra work his mother would have to do washing and mending his things. So he gave her the prize he had won, which was a lovely box of chocolates.

Sparrows in the letter-box

The first time it happened it didn't seem at all funny. In fact, it was rather annoying, and caused Mrs Brewster quite a lot of trouble. One morning, when she collected the newspapers from the letter-box, she found that she pulled out lots of dried grass with them, and it went all over the hall floor.

Now the newspapers are delivered by a boy on a bicycle who whistles cheerfully and has a cheeky face, and I'm afraid that Mrs Brewster blamed him, especially as exactly the same thing happened on the next two mornings when she collected the newspapers.

'I shall have to speak to that young man,' she said. 'I suppose he thinks that stuffing my letter-box full of dried grass is funny.'

She never did speak to him though. On the following day, when she collected the midday post, lots of dried grass was mixed with the letters. Now the postman is just as cheerful as the paperboy, but he is a grown-up man with three children, so he wouldn't want to fill a letter-box with dried grass, would he?

'How on earth could it have got there?' wondered Mrs Brewster. She didn't have to wonder long. That very afternoon, when Bobby came home from school and his mother opened the front door for him, another funny thing happened. A sparrow flew out of the letter-box. It did, really. And when they looked inside it

4

was full of dried grass again. Well, that settled it, didn't it? Sparrows were building their nest in the Brewsters' letter-box.

Of course the Brewsters were delighted. The following morning they got up early, so that they could ask the paperboy and the postman to leave their papers and letters on the mat in the porch instead of pushing them inside the letter-box, where they would get in the way of the sparrows. But they couldn't possibly stand by the front door all day to warn other people as well, could they? So they pinned a very important-looking notice by the flap of the letter-box. This is what it said:

KEEP OFF

SPARROWS AT WORK

PLEASE DELIVER AT THE BACK DOOR

And I'm glad to say that everyone read the notice and the sparrows were left to build their nest without any interference. A very fine job they made of it, too. How many journeys they took to fetch and carry the twigs, dried grass, and feathers I can't imagine, but by the time they had finished their nest was firm and soft and snug, and protected from the wind and rain. In fact it was the ideal place for any father and mother sparrow to bring up a family.

Which is exactly what happened. After a few days Mrs Sparrow seemed to be keeping to her nest most of the time instead of flying about outside, and when Bobby peeped inside the letterbox he saw three light grey spotted eggs.

Then of course extra care had to be taken, and the Brewsters locked and bolted their front door and put up a second notice, in red.

ALL CALLERS AT THE BACK DOOR PLEASE KEEP VERY QUIET AND DON'T RING THE BELL OR KNOCK AT THE FRONT DOOR

Some of the callers were quite alarmed when they read this notice. They tiptoed round to the back door and whispered anxious inquiries in case someone in the house was seriously ill. When they heard the real reason for the notice they were relieved, and news of the Brewster sparrows soon got all over the town, which made Bobby feel quite important. And he felt even more important when he was able to tell people who inquired that the three eggs had hatched out and that mother and three baby sparrows were all doing well, thank you.

Jolly well they did, too, and I'm not surprised. What more could three baby sparrows want than to sit snug in the Brewsters' letter-box all day, while their mother and father brought them delicious food? Peas, and insects, and seeds, and now and then a luscious worm. No wonder they soon grew into strong young sparrows, which

was a pity in a way because they grew too big for their nest and then they learned to fly and the whole sparrow family flew away to another home and left the Brewsters with an empty letter-box. At least, it wasn't exactly empty. It was full of dried grass and twigs, and when Bobby was clearing it out he felt rather sad. But there wasn't any real need for sadness, was there? After all, how could five great big sparrows possibly be expected to go on living in one small letter-box?

And the Brewsters had been very lucky to have them there at all, hadn't they?

Talking to the wind

Do you always remember what your mother asks you to do? Bobby Brewster doesn't, and do you know why? Because he doesn't always listen. Sometimes he sits with his eyes wandering while she is talking to him, and then she says in exasperation, 'Bobby, you're not listening.'

'Yes, I am, Mother,' says Bobby.

'Then what was I saying?' asks his mother.

'Er – I don't know,' admits Bobby sheepishly.

Then his mother always makes the same remark, 'Really, Bobby, I might just as well be talking to the wind.'

There are other times when Bobby only half listens, so although he has heard what his mother said, soon afterwards he has forgotten all about it. Then another conversation takes place like this:

'Bobby, did you remember to put on clean vest and pants this morning?'

'Oh no, Mother.'

'Why on earth not?'

'I forgot.'

And that conversation ends in exactly the same way as before. 'Really, Bobby, I might just as well be talking to the wind.'

Now one afternoon Bobby came home from school, and he hadn't completely forgotten that his mother had asked him to call at the shop, but he wasn't quite sure what she had asked him to buy. So instead of buying a dozen oranges and a tin of sardines, he arrived home with one orange and a dozen tins of sardines.

'Bobby, do you expect us to live on sardines?' asked his mother.

Secretly Bobby thought that might be a jolly good idea, but he said, 'No, Mother.'

'Don't you ever listen properly to what I say?' she asked.

'Sometimes,' said Bobby.

Then the same remark came again. 'Really, Bobby, I might just as well be talking to the wind.'

Bobby felt suitably ashamed of himself and went out into the garden. As it happened a gentle wind was blowing, making a murmur in the trees and a rustle in the long grass at the end of the garden. It was a nice warm breeze, and Bobby sat down on the bank to think.

Then a very funny thing happened. A soft voice whispered, 'Lis-s-sten, lis-s-sten, lis-s-sten.'

'I beg your pardon?' asked Bobby Brewster.

'I s-s-said lis-s-sten, lis-s-sten, lis-s-sten,' repeated the voice.

Bobby hadn't the slightest idea who was talking, but he couldn't help answering, 'I am listening.'

Then the voice said, 'That's-s-s better.'

Then Bobby had a remarkable thought.

'Do you know,' he said to himself, 'Mother keeps telling me she might just as well be talking to the wind, and I do believe that's just what I *am* doing.'

So he asked in a whisper, 'Are you the wind?'

'Yes-s-s,' answered the voice.

'Goodness gracious me,' said Bobby, 'I didn't know you could talk.'

'I can't,' whispered the voice. 'I'm the Wes-s-st Wind and I can only whis-s-sper.'

'Well, that's clever enough anyway,' said Bobby.

'Yes-s-s, but you s-should hear my brother, North,' whispered the voice. 'He howls-s-s.'

'I know,' said Bobby. 'When I was in bed last night I heard him. He sounded horrid.'

'He is-s-s horrid,' whispered the West Wind. 'He's-s-s always-s-s trying to do horrid things-s-s like blowing trees-s-s down and knocking boys-s-s off bicycles-s-s and making people s-s-sea-s-s-sick. I s-s-shouldn't try talking to him if I were you, he'd only be rude.'

'What about your other relations?' asked Bobby.

'Oh, they're all right in their way,' whispered the West Wind. 'Brother S-s-south is gentle, Brother Eas-s-st is s-s-shivery, Cousin North-Wes-s-t blusters, and as-s-s for my Cous-s-sin S-s-south-West, she's-s-s only a girl and s-s-she's-s-s jus-s-st wet.'

'In that case I'll only talk to you,' said Bobby, 'and I can tell when you are blowing by watching the weathercock on top of the church steeple.'

'I can be u-s-s-seful s-s-sometimes-s-s,' whispered the West Wind. 'When your mother keeps-s-s s-s-saying, "You might jus-s-st as-s-s well be talking to the wind," s-s-she's-s-s nearer the mark than s-s-she imagines-s-s. The next time you forget what s-s-she has-s-s as-s-sked you to do, just make s-s-sure that the wind is-s-s in my direction and then as-s-sk me to remind you. I s-s-should be of s-s-some as-s-sis-s-stance.'

'Thank you very much,' said Bobby, 'I'll remember that.'

And he did. The opportunity came on the very next Saturday morning. His mother wanted something that could be prepared quickly for dinner, so she sent Bobby to the grocer's at the last moment. He was in such a hurry that by the time he reached the shop he had forgotten what she wanted him to buy.

'Let me think.' He asked himself, 'What do we usually have for dinner when Mother doesn't want to take too much time? Cold ham? No, that's not it. Corned beef? No, she doesn't like that.'

Then he remembered his friend the wind. He had already noticed from the weathercock on the church that the wind was in the west. The shop was on a corner and the blinds were blowing gently. But first of all Bobby made sure that no

one was watching. He thought it might sound silly if someone heard him asking the wind a question, and I think he was quite right, don't you?

Then he whispered, 'West Wind, what am I supposed to buy for dinner?'

The answer came back clearly and distinctly. It did, really.

'S-s-saus-s-sages-s-s. S-s-saus-s-sages-s-s.'

'Of course,' said Bobby to himself. 'Fancy forgetting that.'

So he went into the shop and bought a pound of best pork sausages. And when his mother cooked them for dinner that day they tasted absolutely delicious.

Which all goes to prove, doesn't it, that there must be magic in the whispering of the wind?

The suitcase

Bobby Brewster was very proud of the new suitcase that was bought for him to use on his holidays. It was made of light brown material that looked like leather but was probably plastic, and was fitted with expensive-looking gold locks. And he was even prouder when, on the day before his holidays, his mother announced that he was old enough to do his own packing for the first time. But before he started she was careful to give him instructions.

'Don't forget,' she said, 'what you need is this: pyjamas – dressing-gown – four pairs of stockings – four shirts – four vests – four pairs of pants – pullover – bathing costume – washing things.'

As Bobby was packing he remembered his mother's list. Then, when he had finished, he pulled the inside strap tight and started to close the lid of his new suitcase.

Then a very funny thing happened. As the lid was closing it made an odd noise. At least, it wasn't exactly an odd noise. It sounded more like a whispered voice. Like this –

'Toothbrush.'

Bobby opened the lid and closed it again. Then the noise – or rather the voice – said it again, this time more distinctly –

'Toothbrush.'

'What an extraordinary thing,' said Bobby Brewster to himself. At least, he thought he said it to himself, but he can't have done, because the voice said, 'There's nothing extraordinary about it.'

'I beg your pardon?' asked Bobby.

'I said there's nothing extraordinary about it,' repeated the voice. 'What really is extraordinary is that you seem to think you can keep your teeth clean for a whole fortnight without a toothbrush.'

'Who are you?' asked Bobby in amazement.

'I'm your new suitcase,' said the voice. 'I'm magic, and what you would do without me I really don't know.'

'You jolly well *must* be magic if you're a talking suitcase,' said Bobby. 'So I shall have to open you up again and see whether I really *have* left out my toothbrush.'

'Of course you have if I say so,' said the suitcase.

And he had. All his other washing things were there – face flannel, nailbrush, toothpaste – but no sign of a toothbrush.

'Thank you very much for reminding me,' said Bobby.

'That's all right,' replied his suitcase. 'Now you can do something for me. I'm sure you're going to have a lovely holiday and I hope the weather keeps fine for you; but what about me?'

'You're coming too,' said Bobby.

'Yes, I know I'm *coming*,' said the suitcase. 'But what sort of a journey am I going to have, and what's going to happen to me when I get there? On the way you will be sitting comfortably in the back of the car. Where shall I be? Probably in the stuffy boot of the car with lots of other suitcases and coats and odds and ends. How would *you* like that?'

'Not much,' agreed Bobby. 'But I'm not a suitcase. Where do you *want* to be put anyway?'

'On the back seat next to you,' said the suitcase. 'And that's not all. When we get down to your cottage in the country, no dark cupboards or dusty lofts for me, if you please. During the holidays I want you to keep me near the window in your bedroom where I can look outside, because I love the countryside just as much as you do. And what's more, I want to go on some trips with you. When you go on a picnic you need a case to keep things tidy, don't you? Well – what about me?'

'I hope Mother won't mind,' said Bobby doubtfully. 'You seem rather smart and grand to use for things like that.'

'That's up to you,' said the suitcase. 'If you're lucky enough to have a magic suitcase, the least you can do is to keep me happy. Then perhaps I might use my magic more often.'

'Very well,' said Bobby. 'I'll see what I can do.'

And he did. His suitcase had a lovely journey down to the country on the back seat of the car and spent a whole fortnight by the window in

the sun. It even went on two picnics. It had been a light brown suitcase to start with, but by the time the holidays were over it had turned a much darker brown through being in the sun so much. And, do you know, on the last day of the holidays that magic suitcase proved to be very useful again. When Bobby thought he had finished packing to go home and was closing the lid, a very funny thing happened.

A voice whispered, 'Dirty shirts.' It did, really. And when Bobby looked in the bottom of his wardrobe there were all his worn T shirts. So he wrapped them up in newspaper and packed them. Just think how annoyed his mother would have been if they had been left behind!

Ever since then Bobby has taken great care of his suitcase and from that day to this he has never forgotten to pack a single thing because it never allows him to forget.

And if that isn't magic I should jolly well like to know what is!

The think balloons

One afternoon, not long ago, Bobby Brewster was at home in the sitting-room reading a comic. It wasn't a very good comic, so he soon closed it up and started thinking.

'Isn't it funny,' he said to himself. 'In comics, when people talk, balloons come out of their mouths with the words in them, like this —

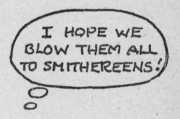

'And when they think, there are balloons over the tops of their heads, with their thoughts in them, like this' —

Then he went on thinking about the same idea. 'Wouldn't it be marvellous,' he asked himself, 'if *I* could really see balloons over people's heads with their thoughts in them.'

His mother was in the sitting-room at the time, reading an interesting book. Bobby folded up his comic and started to stare over the top of her head. Then a very funny thing happened. A thin line shot out of the top of her head and then turned round on itself to form a balloon. It did, really. At first it wasn't very clear, but then some words started to appear inside the balloon. Bobby stared all the harder, and at last managed to read them. Do you know what they said?

Without thinking, Bobby said, 'I'm staring over the top of your head.'

'I beg your pardon?' asked his mother, looking up from her book.

'I said I'm staring over the top of your head,' repeated Bobby.

'There's no need to tell me that,' said his mother in a surprised voice. 'I can see you are.'

Then Bobby realized that she hadn't asked him a question at all. He had actually seen a think balloon over the top of her head.

'This is absolutely marvellous,' he said to himself. 'I can read people's thoughts in their think balloons.'

He could, too. Later that afternoon his father came home from work and Bobby went out to the hall to meet him. There was a think balloon over his head as well. A big one.

I HOPE THERE ARE SARDINE SANDWICHES FOR TEA!

'So do I,' thought Bobby, and even though his mother knew nothing about think balloons, she must have guessed what they wanted, because there *were* sardine sandwiches for tea. And delicious they were, too.

Well, all that evening Bobby went on reading his mother's and father's think balloons. Sometimes it was rather difficult because they were not very distinct and he had to strain to read them, so he got rather tired and went to bed early. When he reached his bedroom he looked in the mirror. There was a think balloon over the top of *his* head in the mirror, but of course the words were backwards, because they were the reflection of his thoughts, you see. They said:

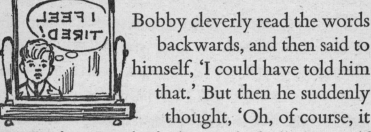

Bobby cleverly read the words backwards, and then said to himself, 'I could have told him that.' But then he suddenly thought, 'Oh, of course, it *is* me, isn't it, so what's the good of telling myself something?' And he quickly went to sleep with his head in a bit of a whirl.

When he woke up the next morning he wondered if he would still be able to see people's think balloons. He didn't have to wonder long. The moment his mother came into his bedroom to get him out of bed he saw one over her head saying:

which was perfectly true, so he bounded out of bed, ate a large breakfast, and ran off to school. At school he felt rather excited. 'This is going to be wonderful,' he thought. 'Masters are going to ask me questions and be thinking about the answers at the same time, and I shall be able to read them over the top of their heads.'

But, you know, it wasn't nearly as wonderful as he had hoped. People have very peculiar thoughts, don't they? Would you like people always to be able to read *your* thoughts over the top of *your* head? Bobby read thoughts he didn't care for at all, some of them not very complimentary. During a lesson one master had a great big think balloon over his head –

That was bad enough, but there was worse to come. Later that day Bobby had to go to Mr Limcano's class. Now, as you know, Mr Limcano is a bit of a magician himself and sometimes he has talked to Bobby about magic things. Well, during Mr Limcano's class that day Bobby thought to his horror that Mr Limcano was beginning to stare rather hard over the top of *Bobby's* head.

'Oh dear,' thought Bobby. 'Am *I* sprouting think balloons and is *he* beginning to read them?' and Bobby couldn't control his own thoughts. He kept thinking, 'Hasn't Mr Limcano got a funny face?' And then he thought, 'Goodness me, can Mr Limcano read my thoughts about his own face?' He got into quite a panic, and as soon as school was over he ran home and sat in a chair all by himself in the sitting-room.

'It's no good,' he said to himself. 'I was quite wrong. Think balloons are not a good idea after all. Somehow or other I must burst this think balloon business once and for all.'

But how was he going to do it? 'How did it start?' he asked himself. 'Of course, I was reading a comic with some think balloons in it, and thought how marvellous think balloons would be in real life.'

Then he glanced on the table. 'There's the very comic,' he thought. He picked it up and opened it out. On the middle page there were lots of pictures of a cowboy adventure, and in the last picture the good cowboy (the one with the white hat) was shooting at the bad cowboy (the one with a black hat), and out of the barrel of his gun was one of those balloons. Can you guess what it said?

The good cowboy must have been a good shot, too, because the bad cowboy in the black hat was hanging over a fence with his mouth wide open and he looked in a very bad way.

'That's an idea,' thought Bobby. 'If a

in a comic can shoot a cowboy in a comic, it ought to work on a think balloon that came out of a comic.'

He went upstairs into his bedroom and looked into the mirror. There was a think balloon over the top of his head in the mirror, but once again, the words were backwards because they were the reflection of what he was thinking.

Bobby pointed his finger, like a pistol, straight at the think balloon over his head in the mirror.

'BANG!' he shouted to himself.

A balloon shot out of his finger in the mirror.

it said. The think ballon in the mirror burst —
and there was a crack right across the mirror
itself.

At that moment Mrs Brewster came into
Bobby's bedroom and saw him standing in a
dazed sort of fashion gazing at the mirror.

'How on earth did that mirror break?' she
asked.

'I was just looking at it,' explained Bobby,
'and it cracked.'

Undressed and in bed

Mr Limcano, who teaches Bobby Brewster at Miss Trenham's School, is a magician. A jolly good one he is, too. He can do the most amazing things, even if he sometimes does get in rather a muddle.

The other day, for instance, he was talking in class about things that people like to happen. Not important things that make history, but little everyday things that make life easier.

'My mother sometimes says after dinner that she wishes the washing up was finished and she was sitting in front of the fire,' said Willie Watson.

'Well, there *are* washing-up machines,' suggested Mr Limcano, 'so you'll have to work hard and save up a lot of money and buy one for her old age.'

'That's a jolly good idea, sir,' agreed the boys.

And, do you know, the more everyday tasks they thought of, the more they found that machines were being invented to perform them.

But trust Bobby Brewster. He thought of something that no machine could ever tackle.

'Late at night,' he said, 'my mother often says that she wishes she could say a magic word and find herself undressed and in bed.'

'Ah,' said Mr Limcano, 'that really *is* something. And, do you know, boys, I *have* got a magic word for it.'

'Oh, sir,' cried the boys, 'what is it?'

'I can't remember off hand,' said Mr Limcano. 'I shall have to consult my magic book.'

So he did. For once his magic book was easily found.

'Here it is,' he said proudly after looking through the pages –

WISCLOPYBED

Then a very funny thing happened. There was a flash, and right in front of the class stood a bed with Mr Limcano lying in it, dressed in his pyjamas.

'That's marvellous, sir,' cried one boy. 'I wish it would work for me like that.'

'I'm afraid that's too much to hope for,' said Mr Limcano from the bed. 'It's a very special magic. Now let's find the antidote.'

And he started looking again in his magic book. But then a worried expression came over his face as he turned from page to page.

'What's the matter, sir?' asked the boys.

'I can't find the magic word to get me up and dress me again,' said Mr Limcano.

'Perhaps there isn't one, sir,' said Bobby Brewster helpfully. 'After all, people often want to find themselves in bed at night, but they hardly ever want to get up in the morning, so no one needs a magic word for it.'

'Oh dear, I hadn't thought of that,' said Mr Limcano. 'What on earth am I going to do? I can't lie here in front of the class in my pyjamas all day. Supposing Miss Trenham comes in. I promised her I wouldn't let my magic get out of hand again.'

The boys made all sorts of suggestions, most of them useless. The most sensible idea came from Bobby Brewster.

'Sir,' he said. 'Wrap a sheet round yourself to make you look like a Roman. Then if Miss Trenham comes in you can be teaching us history.'

Mr Limcano jumped quickly out of bed, and I'm afraid that the boys couldn't help sniggering, although they tried hard not to. Mr Limcano has rather a violent taste in clothes, and he was wearing brilliant red pyjamas covered with black dragons.

However, he quickly twirled a sheet round himself, and not a moment too soon, because there was a knock at the classroom door and in came Miss Trenham.

'Friends, Romans, countrymen,' shouted Mr Limcano in a dramatic voice, and Miss Trenham quickly said, 'I'll see you later,' and went out closing the door behind her, so that was all right.

Well, luckily the bed that Mr Limcano had been lying on was a camp bed, so while he went on with his speech he was able to pack it up with the bed-clothes and put it in a cupboard without too much noise. But not before another anxious moment. Miss Horton came into his classroom to borrow a penknife.

'Friends, Romans, countrymen,' cried Mr Limcano quickly, and Miss Horton said, 'Sorry to interrupt,' and hurriedly withdrew.

So far, so good. But the lesson was due to finish sometime, wasn't it, and how could Mr Limcano go home through the streets in brilliant red pyjamas covered with black dragons, swathed in a sheet, and without anything on his feet?

Then Bobby Brewster had another of his ideas.

What a jolly good thing that boy is so full of ideas, isn't it?

'It's football morning, sir,' he said. 'I don't mind not playing, so if you like you can wear my football clothes.'

'Won't they be rather small?' asked Mr Limcano.

'Well, yes, I'm afraid they will, sir,' agreed Bobby. 'But you can just about get them on except the boots, and they're better than nothing, aren't they?'

'They certainly are,' said Mr Limcano. But he didn't sound very happy.

However, that was the arrangement they made. Bobby ran and collected the football things from his peg, and then Mr Limcano retired behind the blackboard and changed into them. The stockings were far too short and the shorts were too tight, and there was a large gap between the bottom of the jersey and the top of the shorts, but, as Bobby had said, they were better than nothing. And as soon as the bell went for the end of class, the rest of the boys went to fetch their football things. Then they all trooped out of the door and through the school gate at a steady trot, with Mr Limcano at the front.

Miss Trenham was looking out of her classroom window at the time.

'Goodness me,' she thought. 'Poor Mr Limcano will get his death of cold. He must have tried to do his own washing and made all the clothes shrink.' She needn't have worried. As soon as they reached the football ground Mr Limcano asked the boys to start playing amongst them-

selves, and then he rushed home to dress properly, and put on some wellington boots and a large overcoat.

Two other funny things happened that afternoon. Mr Limcano returned to school in his ordinary clothes, so I suppose they must have flown home all by themselves when he said the magic word WISCLOPYBED. And when Mr Limcano arrived at his classroom, Miss Trenham met him and said, 'It was very clever of you to borrow that fancy dress. It will be ideal for our performance of *Aladdin* at the end of term.'

Mr Limcano didn't understand what she meant at first, but then she pointed to the chair by the blackboard.

Do you know what was hanging over the back of it?

A pair of brilliant red pyjamas covered with black dragons!

The whistling golf-ball

On the common up on the hill near Bobby Brewster's home there's a beautiful golf-course. At least it looks beautiful because it is surrounded by trees and bushes and patches of gorse and bracken. Sometimes people who play on it wish it wasn't quite so beautiful. They are always losing golf-balls in the gorse and bracken, and that makes playing golf a very expensive sport.

But for Bobby Brewster it means that a walk on the common is more interesting than ever. Not only can he admire the wonders of nature, but he can also find lost golf-balls, which is a very paying pastime. Found golf-balls can be sold quite easily at 10p. a time, especially to people who don't play very well and often hit the ball sideways by mistake instead of straight forward.

Anyway, one afternoon Bobby was out for a walk by himself up on the common. He took a path through the bracken by the side of the golf-course, and every now and again he looked down on the ground just in case. It was a lovely day and the birds were chirping all around in the bushes.

Then a very funny thing happened. He heard a loud whistle and it sounded like the first notes of 'Happy birthday to you,' like this:

It did, really.

'That's funny,' thought Bobby. 'I've heard some queer bird calls, but never one like that before.'

Then it sounded again, but instead of a whistle it was the same song with special words sung in a squeaky sort of voice.

'Come and find me down here.'

'What on earth is it?' said Bobby to himself. At least, he thought he said it to himself, but he can't have done because a squeaky voice said, 'It's me.'

Bobby looked in the bracken from which the voice had come, and he saw something white partly hidden beneath the bracken.

'Goodness me! It's a small white talking bird,' he said, very surprised.

'No, it isn't,' said the voice, 'it's a small white talking golf-ball.'

'I beg your pardon?' asked Bobby.

'I said it's a small white talking golf-ball,' repeated the voice.

And it jolly well was, for when Bobby looked more closely in the bracken there was a golf-ball, and what's more when Bobby picked it up, it said, 'How do you do?'

'I'm very well, thank you,' said Bobby. 'How are you?'

'Fed-up,' said the golf-ball. 'I've been lying here in the bracken for two days and nights, and I was beginning to think that no one would ever find me.'

'Do you mean to tell me,' asked Bobby, 'that you've been lying there whistling and singing, and no one even heard you?'

'Yes, I do,' said the golf-ball. 'I suppose it's because not everyone is able to recognize magic when they hear it. I'm glad you had more sense.'

'Oh, I often hear and see magic things,' said Bobby. 'There's magic in everything, you know.'

'Even golf-balls,' agreed the golf-ball.

'Yes, especially golf-balls,' said Bobby.

'Well, now you've found me, what are you going to do with me?' asked the golf-ball.

'I don't play golf myself,' said Bobby, 'so I usually sell any golf-balls I find. I can get 10p. for them if they're in good condition. Are you in good condition?'

'Splendid,' said the golf-ball. 'Since you picked me up I never felt better in my life. But don't you go selling me to any Tom, Dick or Harry. I'm a championship golf-ball, and I'm jolly well going to pick and choose who plays with me.'

'I don't see how you can pick and choose,' said Bobby. 'Whoever I sell you to will play with you whether you like it or not.'

'That's what you think,' said the golf-ball. 'If I don't like the look of whoever it is, whenever he puts me on the ground or tees me up and tries to drive, I shall just jump out of the way. I've heard some really horrifying tales from other golf-balls about the way some players treat them.'

'Who, for instance?' asked Bobby Brewster. You see, his father sometimes plays golf, and Bobby knows some of the members of the golf-club.

'Well, Mr Bompass, for one.'

'Oh, him!' said Bobby. 'I'm not surprised. He's a really horrid man, and Father says he's no sportsman. I once played against him on our putting-green at home, and he got in a frightful temper when I won.'

'That's nothing to the tempers he gets in up here on the golf-course,' said the golf-ball. 'All the golf-balls complain about his language. A friend of mine spent a terrible morning with him not long ago. He was almost cut in two. First, Mr Bompass hit over the top of him and sliced his head, and then he nearly drove him into the

ground and cut his other side. But that wasn't all.
After missing him altogether twice, Mr Bompass
picked him up and flung him on to the ground
in a rage. My friend was so disgusted that he
simply rolled away into the gorse and disap-
peared. He was picked up by a boy the next day,
and he's never been the same golf-ball since.'

'I'm not surprised,' said Bobby Brewster. 'I
certainly promise that I won't sell you to Mr
Bompass. In fact, as you are the first magic golf-
ball I ever met, I won't sell you to anybody at all.
I'll keep you for myself. But would you mind

very much if tomorrow I *lent* you to my father?' It so happens that he's playing in a championship match *against* Mr Bompass.'

'Is your father any good?' asked the golf-ball anxiously.

'Sometimes he is and sometimes he isn't,' said Bobby. 'But in any case I promise you he won't fling you on the ground in a rage.'

'Very well,' agreed the golf-ball. 'I'll see what I can do to help him win the championship. I should simply *hate* Mr Bompass to win it.'

'So would my father,' said Bobby.

When Mr Brewster came home that evening Bobby met him in the hall.

'Father,' he said, 'I want you to do something for me.'

'That all depends on what it is,' said Mr Brewster.

'I found this golf-ball up on the common today,' said Bobby. 'It's in jolly good condition, and I want you to use it in your match against Mr Bompass tomorrow. But don't forget I'm only lending it to you. I want it back after the match.' And he handed the golf-ball to his father who looked at it carefully.

'Very well,' he said. 'It looks a very good ball to me. I'll certainly use it and I hope it brings me luck.'

Well, whether it was luck, good form or magic, I don't know, but in that championship match against Mr Bompass the next morning Bobby's father could do nothing wrong. With his first drive the ball sailed down the fairway, pitched on to the green, and he then made a perfect putt for a two. Mr Bompass snorted. Of course not all Mr Brewster's shots were as good as that, but it didn't seem to matter. Whatever he did turned out for the best. And the funny thing was that the luckier Mr Brewster was the more furious Mr Bompass became and the worse he played. In the end, when Mr Brewster putted and by mistake knocked his ball against his opponent's so that it rebounded into the hole, Mr Bompass could contain himself no longer. He picked up his own poor golf-ball in a rage, flung it on to the ground, and shouted, 'I've never known such luck in my life.'

Secretly, neither had Mr Brewster, but he

wasn't going to admit it, and I don't blame him, do you?

Well, needless to say, to everybody's delight Mr Brewster won the championship, and he was presented with a handsome silver cup with his name engraved on the side. As he had promised, he gave that golf-ball back to Bobby, and from that day to this it has been kept safely inside the presentation cup. Which is a sensible place, because it can't roll away, and so it will never be lost again.

The kite

Have you got a kite? They can be jolly good things when they fly, but an awful nuisance when they don't, and I'm afraid that most of the kites I've had myself have not been a great success.

For a time Bobby Brewster didn't have much luck with his kites either. Of course it might have been his own fault because, like me, he was so anxious to get them up into the air that he didn't take enough trouble. You have to be very careful, you know, to put kites together properly and allow the right length of tail, and use them when the wind is suitable.

Anyway, he didn't give up, and perhaps it's just as well, because if he had, I wouldn't have this story to tell, would I?

It all started when the Brewsters were going on holiday, and for some reason or other, for several days before they went Bobby had kites on the brain. Whatever people were talking about, if Bobby was there, they seemed sooner or later to get round to the subject of kites. The Brewsters had kites for breakfast, kites for dinner, kites for tea, and kites for supper. In the end poor Mrs Brewster cried, 'For heaven's sake stop talking about kites, Bobby. I'll *make* one for you to take on holiday if you promise not to mention the word again.'

So he did promise – and Mrs Brewster did make a kite.

I don't know where she got the instructions from, but she must have been a kite expert without knowing it, because it was a real beauty. It was made of red material, with two crossed struts which fitted into pockets at the corners, and a tail of different coloured pieces of paper looped on string. When she had finished it Mrs

Brewster painted two large blue eyes – one on each side of the centre strut, just for fun, and that evening Mr Brewster came home with three large balls of string and a strong piece of stick for winding them on to. Bobby was already excited enough about going away on holiday in any case; but the idea of going away *and* flying his magnificent kite with eyes and hundreds of yards of string made him almost – I said 'almost' – speechless.

At last the great day arrived. The Brewsters drove to the seaside – I forget where they went that year – and even while Mrs Brewster was still unpacking, Mr Brewster and Bobby fitted the kite together and took it out into the field at the back of the cottage where they were staying. It was an ideal place for flying kites – with a stiff sea breeze and no trees, telegraph wires, or chimneys about.

And, do you know, the kite flew without any trouble at all. It was absolutely marvellous. When Bobby let out some string and Mr Brewster threw the kite up into the wind, it soared straight up and the piece of stick whizzed round and round as the kite pulled higher and higher and used up more and more string.

Of course, the trouble with kites that can really fly is that the higher they fly the more winding you have to do when you bring them down. By the time they had let out all three balls of string it was nearly tea-time, and they had to start winding it in again. And winding in string with a kite pulling against it is a tedious business and very wearing on the wrists and hands. Mr Brewster and Bobby had to take it in turns, and by the time they went in to tea, their wrists and hands were so tired through all that winding that they could hardly hold their cups to drink. However, they were both very pleased and Mrs Brewster felt very proud of herself for making the first kite Bobby had ever owned that flew properly.

Well, as you can imagine, immediately after breakfast the next day Bobby went out into the field with his kite again. He was delighted to find that, even without his father, he could get it to fly by throwing it up and running with it into the wind until enough string had been let out to allow it to pull on its own. Once again Bobby let out

all three balls of string, and sat proudly holding
the handle until his mother and father came to say
'Doesn't it fly beautifully?' But then they went
for a walk on the sands and Bobby was left still
holding the handle, and he began to feel rather
bored. After all, there's not much variety in just
sitting holding a kite by its handle, is there? You

can't go anywhere with it because the string might get caught in something, and you can't tie the handle to anything and walk away in case the wind changes, and you daren't let go. Bobby tried pulling in string with his spare hand and then letting it out quickly, but it wasn't very exciting. The kite just dipped and then shot back, with its eyes still staring in the sun. After a time he decided to bring it down and go and find his mother and father. By the time he was ready to follow them, his hands were dangling limply on the end of his arms through so much winding.

On the sands he met a boy and they started talking. The boy had noticed the kite and wondered where it was, and Bobby explained that he had put it away because he was bored with just holding the string.

'Why didn't you send a message up?' asked the boy. Bobby said he didn't know how to send messages up to kites, and the boy explained how to do it.

'You get a piece of paper and make a hole in the middle,' he said. 'Then you let the kite out and thread the stick with the string on it through the hole in the paper – being very careful not to let go of the stick. As long as the hole is big enough and the wind is strong enough, when you pull the string the wind will blow the piece of paper right up the full length of string to the kite. It's great fun.'

'It must be,' said Bobby, and decided to try it after dinner.

So he did – and it was a huge success at first. Pieces of paper wiggled up the string to the kite one after another. But one piece of paper wiggling up string looks just like another piece of paper wiggling up string, and after a time I'm afraid Bobby started to get bored with that too.

Then he had an idea.

'They're supposed to be messages,' he thought. 'If someone kept on delivering blank sheets of paper through my letter-box, I should get rather annoyed. This time I'll send a *real* message.' So round the hole on the next piece of paper he wrote:

PLEASE
LOOP ⬡ LOOP
THE

and sent it wiggling up the string.

Then a very funny thing happened. As soon as the message reached the top of the string, the kite *did* loop the loop. It did, really. Quite a distinct loop. And, what's more, when the kite returned to its normal position, Bobby *thought* he saw one of its eyes wink. He thought he must have been dreaming, so he wrote another message.

And he sent it up the string.

At first the kite kept still, and Bobby was rather disappointed. Then an even more amazing thing happened. A paper message came wiggling *down* the string. It did, really. How it managed to wiggle against the strong wind I can't think, but eventually it reached the bottom and Bobby looked at it. It was the same message that he had just sent up, but on the reverse side of the paper were the words:

91

Bobby added a word to his message to make it read:

and sent it wiggling back up the string. When it reached the top the kite immediately looped a huge loop and then, without any doubt at all, it winked – a great big wink with the left eye.

Well, that settled it, didn't it? Bobby Brewster's kite was magic. And I ask you, what could possibly be better to play with on holiday than a magic kite?

What's more, his kite turned out to be even more magic than Bobby had known at first. Later that afternoon a message came down the string without any warning. This time it didn't just wiggle down. It whizzed. It did, really. Just as if it had been shot from a gun. And this is what it said:

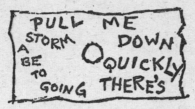

So he did – and only just in time, because no sooner was Bobby safely indoors with his kite than there was thunder, lightning, and pelting rain outside.

That gave Bobby another idea – and a most useful idea it proved to be. For the rest of the holiday, whenever the Brewsters were thinking of going out for the day to bathe, or picnic, or do something exciting out of doors, Bobby took his kite out before breakfast and sent a message up asking:

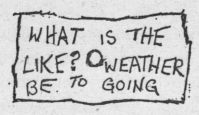

And every time an answer came wiggling down the string saying:

or

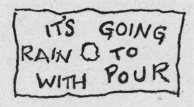

Once it even said:

And Bobby managed to persuade his parents to stay near the cottage for the day. They were most thankful for the warning, because later it really did rain heavily, and they congratulated Bobby on being such a good weather prophet. He didn't tell them that *he* wasn't a weather prophet but his kite was – and do you know why? He kept quiet because he had noticed that the kite only sent messages wiggling down the string or winked its eye when *he* was playing with it by himself, and never when other people were there. So it must have wanted to keep its magic just for him, mustn't it?

There's just one other thing. At the end of the holiday Bobby carefully folded his magic kite away and kept it packed up at home until the next holiday. He didn't want to risk flying it where it might get caught in a telegraph wire, or burned on top of a chimney.

And I don't blame him, do you?